# WHY AM I ON DEATH ROW?

# THE END
# OR THE BEGINNING!

We can become what we were meant to be
at any time during the journey!

# WHY AM I ON DEATH ROW?

## THE END OR THE BEGINNING!

We can become what we were meant to be at any time during the journey!

BY
JIM MAUGHN

Order this book online at www.trafford.com
or email orders@trafford.com

Most Trafford titles are also available at major online book retailers.

Printed in Victoria, BC, Canada.

ISBN: 978-1-4269-2143-8 (Soft)
ISBN: 978-1-4269-2196-4 (Hard)

Library of Congress Control Number: 2009940180

*We at Trafford believe that it is the responsibility of us all, as both individuals
and corporations, to make choices that are environmentally and socially sound.
You, in turn, are supporting this responsible conduct each time you purchase a
Trafford book, or make use of our publishing services. To find out how you are
helping, please visit www.trafford.com/responsiblepublishing.html*

*Our mission is to efficiently provide the world's finest, most comprehensive
book publishing service, enabling every author to experience success.
To find out how to publish your book, your way, and have it available
worldwide, visit us online at www.trafford.com*

*Trafford rev. 12/22/2009*

 www.trafford.com

**North America & international**
toll-free: 1 888 232 4444 (USA & Canada)
phone: 250 383 6864 ♦ fax: 812 355 4082 ♦ email: info@trafford.com

# CAST OF CHARACTERS

CHARLIE ACKERS - What am I doing on Death Row? Poor raising, no money, and easily led down the wrong path. But why? Finally, looked big time trouble in the eye and welcomed help from the past, and, from above.

LADY MARTIN - Early childhood friend of Charlie and Bruce and later, special girlfriend of Charlie. Moved out of the area and became a totally different personality. Revisited Charlie and supported him when the roof fell in.

BRUCE TYLER - A very questionable mentor for Charlie and led him down many shady streets. His early physical and spiritual life, however, were similar to his best buddy. Walked a slippery slope through his entire life.

BARNEY HOWARD - Employed as Chaplain of the state prison. Met and changed many lives. Developed a very different style of soul saving as he met Charlie and his friends.

# WHY AM I ON DEATH ROW?

## THE END OR THE BEGINNING!

# Prologue

Charlie Ackers sits, very depressed, on the bed graciously provided to him by the State Prison. If the surrounding area is not depressing enough, he has no idea what he has done, how he got here, or even if he has any chance of being paroled. Since he has been charged for the suspected act of robbery and murder, he guesses parole is not even an option.

The facts surrounding his capture left him totally puzzled. He had been knocked unconscious at the scene and could remember practically nothing about the event. Was he guilty or innocent?

A trial time has been set by the District Attorney. Charlie's Defense Attorney is struggling to gather correct information in order to prepare reasonable defense. Charlie's attitude is further frustrated by this challenge.

The story continues as Charlie reflects on his past and present while waiting for a visit from the Prison Chaplain, Barney Howard. A prison guard has announced the visit.

# Chapter 1

"Good morning, Mr. Ackers. I'm the Prison Chaplain, Barney Howard."

"What's so good about it? And you can call me Charlie."

"I guess at this point, not much for you. I just wanted to spend a few minutes with you before your trial begins."

"I don't know why, but come on in."

"Charlie, many people have started a day or a trial sitting in a lonely setting, worried about the forthcoming outcome, frustrated to death, and wishing for help. At this moment, from my perspective, your best help can only come from God. He will watch over you."

"What good will that do?"

"At this time you need God's peace. No one knows your outcome, but, whatever it is, you need peace in your heart."

"I'm not sure I've ever had real peace and today is sure a bad time to try to start."

"Just believe me Charlie, God can bring you peace."

The Chaplain had been in this situation many times before, and knew the probable outcome of such a visit. He always wondered what he should have said that he didn't say as he left the side of a prisoner.

The next morning a guard came to escort Charlie to the Court House. As they entered the room Charlie shook from fear and all the unknowns surrounding him. If this was a bad situation for a person fully aware of his actions, how much worse could this be?

The Prosecuting Attorney began his opening address and quickly began to lay serious charges on Charlie Ackers at the feet of the Jury. A Chief Financial Officer had apparently been killed in an explosion and Charlie was found in the same room, very groggy, but very visible as the guilty assassin. A money bag, torn to shreds, with money inside, lay at his feet. Another person within the building had been spotted by a guard, but no identification made.

The Defense Attorney made his opening, but from the start, appeared to be on the fringe of his arguments. His best defensive statements concerned Charlie's past record and his character. This too scared Charlie since he was fully aware of his own record and certainly his character.

What seemed like an eternity for Charlie lasted only about four days. Since Charlie could not remember details, he became tangled up in questions on several occasions. Witnesses within the Finance Office identified no one but Charlie. It did not take a brain surgeon to figure Charlie's days were numbered.

The rest of the trial and verdict were basically details. While much of the evidence was conjecture, and presented in random fashion, the rebuttal of the defense was sketchy, unproven, and as stated before, based on Charlie Acken's prior behavior. As the defense pointed out, however, Charlie had never been involved or associated with such an incident.

With all of this said, the Jury departed and in less than 8 hours, rendered a verdict of "guilty of murder", with a secondary verdict of "attempted robbery". The request to the Judge was a "Death Row" judgment.

Charlie sat in silence. He was shocked, scared, depleted, and wrung out.

The completion of the trial, necessary paper work, and sentencing found Charlie back in Prison, awaiting his move to "Death Row". After a few days, it became apparent that the move might be delayed a short time, subject to some follow up details about a possible appeal. It was quickly decided that the original process would continue and any appeal would have to be handled separately. Death Row would stand unless interrupted by any new results. How long before Charlie would be moved? Nobody knew, but it would happen!

# Chapter 2

Charlie gazed into the small space surrounding him and felt lost and out of touch. The events of the past several weeks had come and gone. The results lingered. While many of the events were recognizable as normal lifetime situations related to Judge, Jury, victims and felons, he honestly felt no attachment to any of these. Where did he fit in this picture? Only time would tell!

Most, if not all, the happenings surrounding Charlie's dilemma had been either told to him by his attorney or observed at the trial. Nothing came from a reach-back in real time to the actual events.

The attorney had laid out the bottom line for Charlie and its cold facts hit like a ton of bricks. 'I couldn't do that', he would say. Then the next significant scene would be addressed and Charlie became more puzzled than ever.

The picture painted before him was one of theft and murder. Charlie stood holding the gun proven, or assumed, to be the murder weapon. Across the room lying on the floor in a pool of blood was the Chief Financial Officer. While the missing money was larger than Charlie's bag of evidence lying beside him, it was enough to nail the motive for the robbery and justification for the killing. In other words, Charlie was caught red-handed with his hand on the weapon and the money at his feet.

The absence of Charlie's friend, Bruce Tyler, at the scene did not register with Charlie until much, much later. Charlie did remember the two of them discussing a trip to the Finance Office to see if Bruce could 'talk his way' into receiving some past due funds that had been owed him. Charlie actually knew very little of the real details.

The first time the so called scheme came up, Bruce had come to Charlie as a person in need.

"Charlie, I need your help."

Charlie had heard these words before, many times. "What's up?"

Bruce began to describe a very convoluted situation. As usual Charlie listened, not really understanding the plan or the need. He wanted to help, but as Bruce continued to describe his dilemma Charlie moved into his usual mode of getting lost in the net results and concentrating too much on the details.

"You see Charlie, I did this project for the bank and time passed. We couldn't get all the material we needed so we had to stall the project for a few weeks. The CFO was not happy with the delay. Along comes A & R Construction from over in Smithville and the big man wants to dump me, and with no pay. I can't stand around and let that happen. I need the money. And he owes me the money."

"What's your plan?"

"I figure if I go in there and lay out my issues and get serious about what might happen if I don't get my money, the man might work things out. And if I tell him I've got someone outside that is coming in to support my case, maybe he'll listen."

"What could I do or say?"

"Well, you don't have to give him a major address. Just using a little threat about what might happen ought to bring him to his senses."

And this was about all Charlie knew on the day the pair made their way to the CFO's office. Charlie waited in the car and Bruce disappeared into the building. The rest of the story unfolded at the trial, but none of it made sense to Charlie.

As time passed he wondered why his 'close' friend had not come to the trial or to make a visit. Then suddenly he realized that Bruce had much to lose by being identified by someone in the building as a participant on that day. While he felt alone in his trouble, he finally understood. In days and years past, he always had Bruce at his side to either create a problem or help him solve one. Now he stood alone in the dark except for the occasional visitor, and sometimes these visits left him more down than up.

Today a now frequent visitor was on his way to chat. Charlie was not exactly thrilled about this pending visit, but would soon make his way to the visitor's station.

Chaplain Howard approached the entrance to the Prison area. Even though prisoner visits were on his regular schedule, he always saved a deeper prayer for the visits with prisoners awaiting more serious circumstances. Something about the atmosphere of doom made it a little harder to handle.

Meetings with Charlie Ackers were beginning to introduce thoughts that did not regularly come to his mind. Sure, it was another golden opportunity to 'win a soul to the Lord'. But, maybe it also had human significance regarding this inhabitant's situation. In any event, there was something different here.

He sat down across the table from Charlie, separated only by a wire screen, and looked him in the eye. "Good morning, Charlie. How's it going today?"

"About the same as the last time you visited. There's not much in here that changes."

"You've got that right. There isn't much that changes, physically. But people do change spiritually, you know".

Charlie was becoming very negative about his situation. His early family life was less than desirable, without discipline, love, or acceptance. His adult life had not been much better. Charlie now felt totally alone and assumed a tough guy role. Today was typical of other days, but, for some reason, Charlie felt more alone than usual. This wasn't going to be a day to make the Chaplain feel good about his visit. Today was going to be real.

"I wouldn't know anything about that. I don't see much in this place that's spiritual, so there's not much room for change since your last visit. And anyway, everybody knows I'm a killer and the God you keep talking about doesn't like killers. Remember?"

"You're right. He doesn't like killing. But, He does like Charlie Ackers, and He can forgive you, even a killer!"

"That's a laugh! Even if I believed in your God, I'm too smart to think he could, or would, forgive me. Nobody else ever would. Why should he?"

"Because that's the kind of God He is. Charlie, He wants to forgive you. He is a forgiving God. He wants to love you. All you have to do is ask Him."

"Nobody's that good! At least nobody I've ever seen. Religion, if it's for anything, is for the Goodies. And I've never been a Goodie. They wouldn't let me even if I had wanted to."

"Who wouldn't let you?"

"Oh, my parents, or the guys in the neighborhood. Nobody! And especially not friends like Bruce."

"Who is Bruce?"

Charlie's mind took a quick flash back to early days. Life was hard. He didn't have many real friends, except Bruce. They grew up together. Later, they partnered in activities, not too favorable with the neighbors. Finally they partnered in activities that led to Charlie's dilemma. Bruce escaped without recognition and momentarily disappeared; however, at this point, Charlie was not aware of the details of Bruce's involvement in the affair.

"Oh, he's just a guy from the past. Nobody really."

"He sounds like somebody important to you."

"Nobody's important to me. Especially not Bruce."

Barney decided it was time to change the direction of the conversation. He inquired some more about Charlie's days as a youth and other early experiences.

"How much time do you have Chaplain? I could keep you here all day talking about my youth. It was so exciting!"

"You tease a lot don't you Charlie?"

"Well I was a youth, not necessarily like everybody else, but still a youth."

"Did you grow up in a small town?"

Well the door was open, so Charlie jumped right in. "I was actually born just outside a very small town. So my space was even smaller."

"Sounds like a rural setting. Just the opposite from my growing up place. Tell me about it."

"It was country, if that makes it rural. I lived on a small farm. My Dad worked in town, but my Mom did some farm work. There were three families who worked the place. I spent most of my younger time with these kids. We worked and played in the dirt, so you can imagine my training."

"Charlie, sometimes people who grow up on a farm have more training than us city folks. It's just different and sometimes gets a bad rap."

"Well if work is training, I had some. Looking back, it wasn't so bad. I guess the thing that changed my attitude and upbringing, both good and bad, was going to the city school. Not a big city school, but at least in the town. Most of the kid's parents worked in town and that gave me a new look."

"Charlie, I've got to move on today, but I want to hear some more. I also want to talk about your move to Death Row. You just don't fit."

"Preacher, that's a tough subject for me. Let's do save it for another time."

"OK. " It was time to end the visit anyway. As usual, the total conversation had to be digested, and also, he had others to see. "I've got to make a few more visits. Enjoyed our talk. If you ever feel I've said anything worthwhile, I sure could use the encouragement."

"You need my encouragement? That's another laugh! Besides, it wouldn't do you any good. My encouragement brings out the worst in people. That's the way I was trained."

"Nevertheless, thanks for the chat. I'll see you soon."

As Chaplain Howard walked away, Charlie's words rang in his ear. It happened every time after a visit. Charlie put on the air of a tough guy, mad at the world, and not caring. But somehow, he just didn't fit the picture. As he continued to walk, these thoughts turned over in his mind. He wanted to set up a small separate investigation, but he knew things would move slowly. Maybe one day we will figure it out. But he realized time was passing and, sooner or later, time would run out.

Back at his office, Chaplain Howard continued to play the possible events of Charlie's situation over and over. It interfered with his daily work and he knew that he either had to delve into the affair big time or get it off his mind. He doubted seriously, that the latter was a possibility. After all, what are Chaplains in a prison for?

He had some preliminary information, knew he had a long way to go. One path that needed big time study was a close review of the trial. He decided to take a day off from his routine and spend it at the Court House.

Lack of available data and privacy concerns would be a stumbling block; however, he would push it as far as possible. Suddenly, he had a great idea. Everyone watched criminal investigations and jury trials in the newspaper, radio, and now on Television, even in fictional shows. What might he learn from such investigation?

And so, wound around his daily necessary routines, the Chaplain made time to explore the factual and fictional world of crime and it's treatment of suspected criminals. He admitted to himself that he was on a very slippery slope, and probably wasting valuable time, but he had to pursue his idea. It was, at this point, all he had. He had to answer the question, "Why was Charlie headed to Death Row?"

# Chapter 3

A little time passed and the Prison guard came to Charlie's cell with word of yet another visitor.

"I don't want another visitor or another sermon."

"You might change your mind when you see this one!"

"What's the name?"

"Lady Martin. Quite a looker!"

The name Lady Martin set off a flow of memories from his childhood. The little town where he eventually went to school. His old house with the chickens in the back and the homemade swing sitting in the yard. His parents, who never seemed to have time for him. In reflection, now he understood their problem. Work all day and raise a little money had to be the goal, not raising children. Even though he never used her real name or even thought about it, he did remember, in the earliest of days, her real name was not Lady.

Charlie moved to his chair behind the wire screen. He was nervous and excited at the same time. He could not believe "Lady" Martin was paying him a visit. Lady grew up in the little town, but also raised in a poor family. They had been sweethearts at one time; however, Lady had moved on, become well educated and, apparently. successful. He thought about her occasionally, when the going really got rough. He thought to himself. How much rougher can it get?

"Charlie, I'm glad that you permitted me to visit you. How long has it been since I've seen you?"

"It has been a long time. I can't believe you wanted to visit me. As a matter of fact, why did you come?"

"To be honest, I'm not sure. All I know is that something or someone kept urging me to come. Maybe it was God. What do you think?"

"One thing that I think is that I don't think much about God. And the last time I saw you, you didn't either."

This opening gave Lady an opportunity to share a little with Charlie. She became excited at the thought. "Charlie, that has changed! The life we lived a long time ago seems so far away now. I am not the same girl you knew then."

In some ways you still are. You're still beautiful! I always thought you were a super person, even though I would never have told you. You know, you are the only good thing that ever happened to me."

"Why wouldn't you tell me? You know that I felt very close to you. We shared many happy experiences."

At this point, Charlie had to do a gut check. This conversation might cause him to drop off his high and mighty position and admit caring and concern. "I just couldn't bring myself to do it. I never could measure up. It wouldn't have worked. You were too special. Much too special for a bum and a loser like me."

"Charlie, I am special, now, at least in God's sight. And, so are you!"

Charlie shifted in his seat, took a deep breath, and quickly regained his original stance. He knew he must head this conversation off somehow. "Is that what you came here to tell me?"

"Well, yes it is. At least that's part of it. How did you know?"

"The Preach around here has been laying that same sermon on me. Sometimes I almost believe it."

"You should Charlie, you should!" Once again Lady tingled with excitement at the though of helping poor Charlie. "When we were kids, and even later, I knew something was missing in our lives, but it took me a long time to figure it out. And I want you to figure it out too."

"I'm not very good at figuring anything out, especially since I entered this world."

"Charlie, you don't remember me as a person believing in God or trying to be close to him. But before we went our separate ways I knew something was missing. Several of the kids I knew had struggled with the same issues and some had finally figured out that God can help us all and really wants to."

"You didn't seem any different."

"I really wasn't different around you. I guess my feelings for you got in the way. I knew I was missing something and now I believe that was a major issue with our relationship."

Charlie realized that this conversation was going in the wrong direction. Continuing his approach to keep Lady's caring at a distance, Charlie began his usual sermon of 'leave me alone'.

"Why me? Why don't people just leave me alone and let me die in peace? I am not interested in using up all my energy worrying about what's missing in my life. What could possibly be missing in an environment like this? I've got it all!"

Ignoring his intention, Lady laughed out loud. "Charlie, you're still funny! I remember that about you. You made me laugh all the time, although sometimes it was at my own expense."

Charlie realized that Lady was defusing his arrogance. But he couldn't help himself. "I was pretty mean in my day", he said with a smile. "In fact, I didn't like people too much. And they liked me about the same!"

"I liked you, Charlie. And I still do, but in a different way. And I want you to like me and believe what I tell you. Can I come back to visit soon. Could I?"

"Sure you can. I wouldn't stop you anyway, if you really wanted to come. "

"But I hope you want me to come. I'll see you again in a few days."

Charlie watched the best thing that had ever happened in his life disappear down the hall. In his heart he did not want her to leave. In his head, he breathed a sigh of relief, and slumped back in his chair.

As Lady Martin left the Prison, she realized that there had been no conversation about Charlie's situation. She guessed that the long period of separation had to be closed before that subject surfaced.

She could not get Charlie off her mind as she drove away from the Prison. Her memories of the past times were just as vivid and confusing as Charlie's. One morning as kids were gathering outside school, Lady ran into a few of her buddies. Charlie was there but seemed to be captured by something or someone from another world. Lady finally worked her way over toward Charlie.

She had been on a Youth Retreat the weekend before and realized there was information she had learned that needed to be shared with Charlie. Lady began to set up dialog with several around her, but could not seem to capture Charlie's attention. She pondered his condition and uttered to herself, "What is he thinking about?"

Finally, she looked straight at the boy with every intention of delivering some spiritual message, particularly to Charlie. Charlie glanced her way and wondered what she was up to. His demeanor looked like a block of ice to Lady. At the last moment, she totally changed her 'sermon' and drifted into silly comments about school lessons. A few minutes later Charlie eased out of the gathering and on to some unknown activity, likely something not necessary to reveal to the general public.

As Lady moved from the yard into the schoolhouse, she felt depressed and upset. "Why did I let him get away? I had my chance and blew it!"

She knew at some point she wanted to lead Charlie down a different road, but for whatever reason it had never happened. She never reached the 'pulpit' with him as a youth and he continued to sit in the empty pew. For this Lady was truly sorry.

Thinking to herself she admitted that Charlie's continued getting into trouble and putting other things in the way of their relationship, caused her to move away. She muttered to herself, "What a shame that history cannot be revisited! And why in the world is Charlie headed to Death Row?"

# Chapter 4

Lady's visit had stirred many memories of the past. Some good and some not so good. He remembered the first time he actually thought about Lady as a real woman. A beautiful young lady, appropriately named! He couldn't remember exactly how old he was, but he was old enough.

Charlie drifted into a trance of the past. He had wormed an afternoon job out of Smokey, at Winter's Market. The job was tough and paid very little, but it was a job. In reality, Smokey was not his name; however, based on the magnitude of cigarettes smoked and no telling what other tobacco products, he had become Smokey to the neighborhood.

Halfway through the afternoon, with sweat pouring down his face, he moved a couple of boxes to the front porch of the store. Breathing a sigh of relief, he looked up and there she stood. Charlie had seen her before, many times. They had played together as children. They had gone to school together until Charlie dropped out. They had dated a few times and he had seen her here and there. They ate a meal and took in a movie now and then. But here she was, as though he had never seen her. He could not believe his eyes.

"Hello Charlie. You look tired. Are you OK?"

"Hi Lady. You look wonderful. Are you OK?

Lady was accustomed to Charlie's tactics, so she continued without a blink. "Are you sure you're OK. I've never seen you look like this."

"I've never seen you look like this either! What have you done to yourself?"

"Charlie, you're changing the subject. Be honest with me. I'm concerned about you."

"I'm fine Lady. I'm just worn out from this 'soft job' I have. But I'm alive enough to see a beautiful woman in front of me and I like what I see."

"Well, aren't you nice. I don't think I look any different today than I did yesterday."

"You do to me. But I think it might be me and not you."

"What do you mean?

And so a brief romance started. Pleasant at first, but then as Charlie became more involved with work and an occasional, not so ethical project, Lady's love interest in Charlie waned. She did continue to count him as a friend. Charlie did not understand the change in her. He still believed he loved her very much. But she was different!

All these thoughts about the latter days of their relationship then stirred memories of earlier days. To call Smerna, small town America, would be a stretch, but nevertheless, this was the case. One of the few miracles in Charlie's young life was the existence of a 'real high school' there that was later available to him. It wasn't clear why the small country elementary school existed near Charlie's home, but it did, and this too was a blessing unaware.

Many students left the education process at the end of the 8th grade. Thus was the case with Bruce, even though he tried reentry a couple of times latter on, much to no avail. As best as Charlie could remember, the final straw broke when Bruce was offered a 'high paying' job opportunity in town. Bruce lived about a mile from Charlie, but, travel to town for him never seemed to be an issue. Fortunately for Charlie, his education was able to continue.

The family did not move to town, but transportation was available through hiking, bikes, and occasionally through a necessary trip to town for groceries by his Dad.

Since Lady lived in town, she obviously went to the city school. Charlie's first encounter with her as a young youth was on the second day he attended the new school. They were in the same class and. as fate would have it, she sat in front of him. The teacher was bearing down on a tough subject and Charlie was getting lost. Finally, he tugged on her sleeve and whispered, 'help'! As soon as possible she came to his rescue, and this process became a normal, almost daily, activity. Charlie was grateful for her help and she seemed happy to be helpful

"Charlie, do you study much at home?" Her observation, even as a young person, was that Charlie did not save much time for study.

"I don't have much time to do school work", he answered.

"I thought so. You need lots of help. Why don't you get your Mom to help."

"My Mom doesn't know much more about school than I do."

"Charlie, that's ugly. You know better than that."

"I don't mean to be ugly. She just does lots of work on the farm also."

Perhaps, Lady understood his situation at that moment, must better than the average small child. She never brought the subject up again and she always helped where she could.

Suddenly, Charlie awoke from his trance. Pleasant thoughts of his relationship with Lady, both young and older, were easier to dream about than thoughts of her latter rejection of him, as a boyfriend. Suddenly, Charlie was back in the real world, and, as usual, it wasn't very pleasant, and Death Row was looking him straight in the face.

# Chapter 5

A few days later Charlie found himself walking to the same seat behind the same wire screen. He talked to the guard as he walked. "Why do they keep coming? Why can't people just leave me alone? All it does is remind me of what I don't have."

While his words were true, he could not help but feel his heart had been touched. But why did people continue to come see him? What could he possibly have to offer anyone, let alone from this vantage point? And this visitor had requested that his name be withheld. Unknowns are now coming!

"Right over here, Mr. Tyler." The guard motioned for the guest to sit down.

Charlie took a second glance when he realized that his new guest was Bruce Tyler, his boyhood friend and adult accomplice. 'What does he want'?

"Hi ya Charlie, ole boy. Glad to see ya. Planned to get here sooner, but you know how it is, business and all."

"No, I don't know how it is any more." Charlie's voice made his demeanor very clear. "My busy-ness is down right predictable. What do you want anyway?"

"I thought you might like a visit from an old friend. We are still friends, aren't we Charlie?"

"Seems to me you wouldn't care if we were or not. What's in it for you?"

"What kind of attitude is that? After I come all the way out here and on such a busy day too!"

The anger in Charlie's heart surfaced to his mouth as the conversation continued. "Maybe it's guilt, Bruce. Maybe you came out here to ease your conscience. To see how good I've got it so you can sleep at night. Is that it?"

"I don't know what you're talking about. I don't understand why you are so mad." Suddenly, Bruce realized that their comments might be heard. He wasn't sure about being recorded, however, he knew he must watch his step, and his mouth.

"Do I sound angry? Why should I be angry? Maybe unlucky, but not angry!" He knew how unlucky he had been when the guard accidentally stumbled upon him in the Finance Building and how lucky Bruce had been that no one found him. Charlie also knew that Bruce must be careful to keep his record clean. "I've tried to shake the past, Bruce, but I can't seem to shake it. Looks like you haven't either."

"What do you mean?" Bruce was a little uneasy at this point.

"If I was in your shoes, I don't believe I would be here. I'd still be off in the Caribbean, somewhere, living it up, not visiting scum like me in prison."

"How did you know I spent some time in Jamaica?"

"The same way you knew I spent some time in here. Word travels far!"

"You got it all wrong, Charlie. I just spent some time alone, trying to get my house in order. You know how it is."

"You seem to think so."

"Time is up, Mr. Tyler." The guard motioned for Bruce to leave.

Bruce breathed a sigh of relief at the chance to end, for now, this uncomfortable conversation. Between Charlie's anger, and the need to keep the wrong words off the table, the stress level began to sizzle. "See you next week, Charlie."

These parting words caused Charlie to ponder. Why was he coming again, and so soon? Bruce had been very fortunate to apparently miss the terrible scene where Charlie was or, at least escape the building before he was identified. He couldn't blame Bruce for protecting himself at the moment. Something was up, however, and time would likely reveal it. He knew Bruce was not making social calls. Well, he would wait. What else did he have to do? In the meantime, there had to be some insight into what actually happened on that fateful day.

Drifting back again into earlier days, Charlie remembered times when the two of them actually supported each other in good, and not so good, situations. When Charlie went to high school and Bruce went to work, their ventures together seemed to increase over earlier days. Part of this likely was growing older and having more freedom. Some of it however, created problems for Charlie since education created the need for night time study and Bruce's working daytime left his night rather open.

On several occasions, Charlie remembered being tardy with his homework due to some illustrious venture on the previous night. Most of the time the activities were bland, but occasionally they got a little out of hand. One night Bruce conjured up a story about removing some fruit from the back storage of a competitor of ole Smoky Winters. Smokey ran the best market in town and it always helped to bond with the best. It sounded exciting and if it helped Smokey, why not try it? As usual, Bruce made the distraction for the store owner while Charlie escaped with the loot. Charlie could remember several such instances, but somehow had not associated these kind of pranks with the one that had him behind the bars.

Bruce walked at a fast pace as he left the visiting room. The sight of the place created a fear in him. 'This place gives me the creeps. Poor ole Charlie.' As he walked he wondered about the day of the trouble. 'I never thought he'd wind up like this. It wasn't my idea. Why is he headed to Death Row?'

# Chapter 6

After all the company for the week, Charlie hoped that this might be a day he could just be alone and, maybe, even relax a little. Obviously people did not find themselves in prison to relax, but here he was, so why not take advantage of it. The atmosphere of his accommodations, however, did not lend themselves to very pleasant thoughts so relaxing shifted to more thinking.

Sitting on his bench, he reflected on his past visitors. They just walk in here and walk right out again. There's no justice. Quite a revelation for a person in Prison! Almost funny how you take things for granted.

For a moment he thought ole Bruce was talking straight. He still had the charm and the gift of gab. It had been so long and the facts were all mixed up.

Charlie began to think about the past again. He remembered the old neighborhood. People didn't know how poor they were. Fun was where you found it. Shoot those baskets until the rim would ache and the net would burn. Drag down to Smokey's Market and either cheat him out of a soda or steal one, if necessary. After all, trickery worked in both directions. If you help a guy, you ought to be able to recover some of his profit. A great philosophy! Bruce was always better at the ruses than Charlie. Charlie always got distracted. He knew that. He knew how Lady always got his mind out of socket. And Bruce would take advantage of it!

Charlie's entry back to the past was not as exciting as before, but he did have some good times, as well as some bad, in those days. Seemed as though ole Bruce was always in the plot somewhere. He really didn't have any other close friends, except Lady, so, ole Bruce it was. It should have been an omen to the future that all the tricks and schemes they pulled off would eventually lead them to disaster. But, as often happens, it didn't.

In the small neighborhood where Charlie hung out, as time passed he was more and more isolated with Bruce. Charlie was very prone to become an 'employee' under Bruce's leadership and the resultant pay was not worth the effort. But it continued!

How the boys escaped the local police time and time again was a miracle. All of their capers were not illegal, but Charlie began to wonder if even the fun times were really worth the effort. Fortunately, at some point it became obvious that Charlie must find honest work. This did not please Bruce, but even he finally realized some money had to be earned the hard way.

Time passed! Sometimes the two worked together, sometimes separately. This tie, along with all of the earlier activities, was primarily responsible for the beginning of the end possibilities.

On some occasions, Bruce would set Charlie up in what appeared to be a perfect scheme. Bruce would engage Smokey in conversation, get him out in front of the store and then Charlie would make off with $5 from the register. He won't ever miss it. A typical lie from the master! The plot worked well until one day Lady appeared on the scene and so diverted and confused Charlie that he walked right into Smokey coming back into the store. The $5 bill glowing in his right hand looked like a torch. The rest is history!

Somehow in all of Charlie's memory swings, he never really dealt with how different he and Bruce were. They spent a lot of time together. Got into a lot of trouble together. Chased the same girl occasionally. But in reality, Bruce and Charlie lived on opposite sides of right and wrong. To Charlie, Bruce's deceptions were fun, not crooked. He really never set down and thought about their outcome until it was over and too late. And for some strange reason, he never seemed to associate yesterday's trouble with today's actions. Bruce, on the other hand, calculated the risks for every move and made sure that his accomplish was usually in the gap between himself and trouble.

As Bruce said one day out on the corner waiting for his buddy to arrive, 'Man cannot make enough money strictly working as a 'grunt'. We've got to either get a real job or work out a real 'Plan'. And thus the final caper was designed by Bruce and messed up by Charlie and nature."

Back in real time, Charlie's memory of recent events continued to be blurry most of the time. He muttered to himself. I can't blame it on Lady or Bruce this time. At least not until recently. Why can't I just remember? I stay so mad and angry and frustrated. Bruce knew that would happen. Why didn't I just shake him, like Lady wanted me to do. No, I thought I could do it better. And it cost me my girl. Big deal! Now it's costing me my life. That job was so simple, but it all went wrong. Almost too wrong. What happened? I've got to remember. I've just got to.

Not that it would do him any good, but Charlie also wondered why he had not been moved to Death Row. 'Why am I thinking about this?', he muttered to himself. 'If this place isn't bad enough, just think what a move will bring. From bad to worse!'

# Chapter 7

Charlie began to feel like he was hosting special guests almost every day. While the Chaplain was not a part of his past, he had taken on the role of a close friend. At least closer than anything else in this God forsaken place. And having Lady and Bruce around took him back to yesteryear and raised memories that had not surfaced in such a long time.

The little farm where Charlie grew up was really not that far from the so-called city and as time passed Charlie spent less time at home and in the small surroundings he was familiar with. It didn't take long to get oriented and feel a little at home in new surroundings.

Even though Lady had grown up in small town USA, she was not present or informed on many early activities the two boys shared. And, as Charlie learned later on, this turned out to be helpful in maintaining a good stance with the lady when the activities moved more to serious issues. Also, perhaps these early activities, which were less significant, caused Charlie to underestimate the severity of later ones.

It was a miracle, however, that both boys were not incarcerated long, long ago. While some of their adventures weren't really that bad, some, involving money, took on the guise of theft in a strong way and they both admitted their luck at escaping the rope.

One such event was planned for quite a while. A Western Union van arrived in town about twice a week. Normally the van was filled with bushels of paper work and only a few live jobs were represented. Bruce discovered through some loose conversation from an acquaintance that, on certain trips, money normally being exchanged through the wires was transferred instead, live and on wheels. To pin down the specifics of this news took some time, but was finally nailed down.

On a particular Saturday, the van arrived on schedule and parked in an alley beside the local bank.

"Charlie, I think that's it. Get over here closer."

Charlie moved to his new position and gazed in awe at the arriving van.

"Bruce, how much money do you think we can get? What if we get caught?"

"You ask too many questions. Just be still and let's see what happens."

The van parked in an alley between the bank and a mercantile store. The two guards disappeared into the bank.

"Ok, Charlie, when I break this glass, grab that door handle."

"Won't it make a lot of noise?"

"Just pay attention and we'll be alright."

It was very obvious that Charlie's fear of capture was much stronger than his desire for the money, even though he could certainly use it. Bruce, on the other hand, tuned in to the opportunity before him and fear had to come later.

The boys helped themselves to as much money as they could find in the few minutes they had to search. There really wasn't that much, but every little bit helps, or at least that was Brice's philosophy.

"Hurry up Bruce. They'll be here any minute."

"I'm hurrying. How about do what I ask and just shut up."

Just as the two boys were leaving the scene, one of the guards arrived and spotted them moving away from the van. To make a long story short, only a miracle saved the day. The guard had to decide between taking on the boys or calling on his buddy for help. He chose the boys and just as he made a lunge for Bruce, his foot slipped and he came face down on the bumper of the van. He was out cold.

The rest of the story is obvious. While the boys didn't make a fortune, it was a fruitful venture and the money came in handy as usual. By the time the second guard arrived, Bruce and Charlie were far enough away from the scene to avoid spotting and thus endeth the day. Such action on Charlie's part would have spoiled many happy days with Lady had she known about the event. Looking back, Charlie now remembered the comparison between his luck on that day and his dismal luck that placed him near Death Row. And he still didn't know what that luck was.

# Chapter 8

All of these visits and brief glimpses back into their earlier days added even more confusion to Charlie's everyday life. What was life really like in the early days and how did it tie into the terrible situation he was now in? Are these people friends or enemies?

Charlie was born in the country near the little town of Smerna, not far from the big city of Maconville. His Dad had two jobs, one as a part time manager for the old man down the road who owned most of the property. His other job, which began in mid afternoon and continued until almost bed time, was in a little garage on the edge of Smerna. Charlie's Mom kept the house, worked on the farm as necessary, and canned fruit and vegetables from the close by garden. To say these two parents were busy would have been a gross understatement. When did they ever have time for a son?

Charlie had become use to the situation very early and spent a great deal of time by himself. History has revealed that this situation is both helpful and harmful. As time passed he became available to work the farm along with his Mom. Time in the country moved slowly and having parents always busy left him looking for playmates along the way.

One such playmate was Bruce Tyler. Bruce's situation was even worse than Charlie's, if that was possible, and perhaps that is what started the tie between them.

Finally when school loomed on the horizon, the two boys were able to leave the confinement of the country and venture near Smerna proper. The distance was close enough for walking when necessary and that was almost every day. As time passed, both boys dreamed of ways to make the trip on wheels and avoid the dust and rain. The dreams did not mature right away.

School to these boys was a curse and a blessing. During school physical work was avoided, but mental work was necessary. It wasn't that they were dumb, it was more that they were lazy, or needing rest, a result of many early days working their shoes off.

"There must be a better way to make a living than what out parents are facing", repeated Bruce almost every day.

"I wish I knew what it was", echoed Charlie.

"We got to do better than this and school is so boring."

And so the chain was started. A need for transportation, a need for money, and a need for relaxation. Somehow school got lost in all of this.

Very early in grammar school a young girl by the name of Gladys Martin entered the picture. Obviously at this age, only as a friend, but to Charlie, a special friend. Somehow, she brought with her an elegance that Charlie had never witnessed. Bruce thought she was cute, but mostly Bruce liked friends he could beat out of money or whip into shape to follow him.

It wasn't long until Charlie and Gladys had developed quite a friendship. Charlie did not enter her house until much later, but the two of them managed to play and even study a little. Maybe school wasn't so bad after all!

One day as the two of them were walking along a path behind the school, Charlie asked, "Who are you named after?"

"Why, I'm named after my grand ma. Why do you ask?"

"I don't know. I'm just not used to names like that in my family."

"Does it bother you, Charlie?"

"No, not really. I just don't think of Gladys when I see you."

"What do you think of then?"

"You really want to know?"

"Yes, I do!"

"I think of, Lady!"

"Then why don't you call me Lady? I think it's a great name for me."

And so the name was changed for the two of them and never again did Gladys enter the picture. It wasn't clear how the girl's parents reacted to the change, but in a sense, the two kids never really cared.

Much time passed and about the 8th grade Bruce decided he had had enough education. Charlie and Lady tried to talk him out of it, but he wouldn't listen. And there was also pressure from home to work more.

Charlie made it to the 10th grade and, primarily due to an accident, his Dad had to cut out his mechanic job. Charlie had learned enough from talking and watching to hang on and so decided to take over the job. He did pretty good and he did have his Dad to mentor him occasionally. But, alas, education for him too was over.

Lady was not happy with either situation, especially Charlie's. "You have to graduate from High School", she would say.

"Why", Charlie would ask. "I know a lot."

"One day you will be sorry, that's all."

Now, with this early history behind them, the two boys became even closer. Some good things and some bad things resulted from this relationship. Charlie had a good heart, but was often swayed to go-along with many stupid, and sometimes dangerous, escapades.

Time passed and Bruce's parents moved out of the territory. Bruce followed them for several years, but would occasionally return to the little town to see his buddy.

Lady finished high school and moved on to attend college. She too, would come back to visit her parents and also occasionally locate Charlie. The two still maintained their friendship, but absence is a strain on relationships.

Each time Lady saw Charlie, she tried to get the nerve to speak to his religious situation. But, each time, either Charlie's attitude or her shyness of the subject, kept the topic off the table. She always left sorry for another failure.

At some point Bruce and Charlie broke their tie, more again from absence than from issues. Some of Bruce's activities, however, took on a more serious criminal type nature. Charlie, meanwhile, was not aware of these activities. In any event, it had been quite a while since the two of them were together when Bruce showed up to partner one more activity with Charlie. Woe be that day!

Finally, back in real time, Charlie lay on his bed reflecting on all these past moments and still trying to put the big Death Row puzzle together.

# Chapter 9

A couple of days passed and the Chaplain returned for another visit. As usual, Charlie sat with mixed emotions as he approached.

"Good morning, Charlie. I've been thinking a lot about your situation."

What an entrance thought Charlie! What do I say in return? "Well guess what? So have I."

"I'm sorry Charlie. Let me clear this up. I'm talking about how you got here; your past and the events of your arrest."

"And so what?" Charlie stayed with his attitude, but deep down his emotions trembled. What is the Chaplain up to? And why?

"I don't have it put together just yet, but I will. I've been around prisons a long time and, well, you just don't fit the typical 'crook'. In the meantime, I've been reading the Bible again and I've got another story to tell you."

"I'd rather hear more about my situation, but since I'm going to hear the Bible story, let's get it over with." Again Charlie was afraid his looks would betray his real feelings.

"This story involves two guys who wind up in prison. They are Paul and Silas or, as you might say, missionaries. They are doing the Lord's work and land in jail. What do you think their attitude might be?"

Well, my attitude ain't so good and I probably deserve to be in here. If I knew for sure I was innocent, I would make a lot of noise."

"You've opened up the punch line to my story. These guys didn't deserve to be in jail, and yes, they did make a lot of noise. They were able to praise God in the middle of their problem and even led some of the jailers to God."

"I can't imagine me leading anyone to God, much less any of these nuts who work here. That's a laugh!"

"Well, you never know what God is going to accomplish with our circumstances. Time will tell!"

"That's a good motto for this place, Chaplain. We've got nothing but time. You're a riot!" Charlie laughed at his own comment, but deep down he would later admit to himself that the Chaplain's words caused a stir within him.

"See you next, time, Charlie!"

As the Chaplain walked away, Charlie's thoughts drifted, for the first time, to the possibility that he might not deserve to be headed to Death Row. What a revelation! What if the Chaplain was right? Without any information, these thoughts caused more concern than relief, but at least he was looking down a different road than before.

What Charlie was really dealing with was a combination of issues and feelings. The human issue was, of course, his physical destination as he wrestled with a Death Row possibility. Well, at this point it wasn't a possibility, it was a reality.

The spiritual issue was seeping into his thoughts on a daily basis. While he didn't really know what he believed, he was filled with the thoughts of not being a good enough person to deserve God's benefits. 'How could God like me?' he would ask himself. Lady, and the Chaplain, worked on this issue, but Charlie had a long record of other thoughts to deal with before this issue was settled. He did wonder, however, why he had not, at some earlier time, been exposed to some of this religious conversation. He couldn't blame anyone, certainly not his parents. After all, he had a busy life and a man, or boy, could only handle so much. But, in retrospect, a little of it along the paths he and Bruce often took, might have made a difference.

In the meantime it appeared that Death Row might over shadow God and win out in this battle. But, maybe the Chaplain would have some good news for him down the road.

# Chapter 10

At some point the routine of the prison began to wear on most residents and Charlie Ackers was no exception. Day after day, the same dismal scenery, the same hard work details, and the same down trodden inhabitants. Words really could not describe the condition of the prison or the depression it caused. He did realize, however, that maybe this place was a blessing compared to where he was headed.

In a sense, he surprised himself on this day when he was notified he would have a visitor. He was almost thankful to get the word. When the visitor's identity was revealed, he even managed a smile, to himself.

"Lady, I wasn't sure you'd come back. I wasn't very pleasant before."

"I understand Charlie. If I were in your shoes, I wouldn't be very pleasant either."

"Oh, I bet you would. I don't ever remember you not being pleasant. Even when you were mad at me, you were pleasant."

"I have more reason to be pleasant now. And I know you don't feel comfortable talking about this 'God' stuff. But you need to hear it!"

"I do? How are you so sure?"

"I'm just sure. More sure of that than anything in this world. I can't believe I've waited so long to talk to you about God.

"What was the rush?"

"Charlie, we never know what the future will bring. And even in your situation, God can lift you up and hold you tight."

"Wait a minute! You're getting a little far out for me. What are you trying to say?"

"We'll get to that, but first let me tell you about my talk with the Chaplain."

"I figured you two would find something to talk about."

"Well, we did. But something different than you're thinking about. We've been talking about you!"

"Me? Why me? I'm not a hot topic of conversation, at least not compared to your God topic."

"You are a very hot topic of conversation; at least for us you are. We are interested in your story, as well as your future."

"My future is about as interesting, and as long, as that roach over there against the wall." Charlie paused long enough to encourage the roach to head off in another direction. "Don't be frightened. He won't come over your way. Besides, you're too clean for a roach to be interested in you."

"Charlie, you remembered our experiences with roaches." Lady was touched, even if the subject was a little off beat. "How sweet! But let me finish.

Barney, I mean the Chaplain, thinks there are some unusual, and missing, facts about your situation. He wants to help you. And, so do I. Charlie, why did you get yourself into so many bad situations when you were young? You know all of that, helped lead to this!"

"It probably did, but that's history now. Nobody can help me in this one! At least not like you're talking about. I'm here and I'm going to be here until they move me and make me take the walk."

"Why were you at that Finance Building that night? Who was with you? What really happened? We might be able to help."

"Lady, get real! You can't help me. Not with this. Nothing good can happen to anyone involved with me."

"I'm willing to take a chance, Charlie. We go back a long way. And I was sweet on you, you know! I still care about you and I can't sleep at night knowing you do not know your God."

These words touched Charlie as he had not been touched in many years. Sure, he and Lady had a relationship. But that was many moons ago. He lost her then. She can't possibly want him now. She doesn't need to waste her time with him. 'But. here she is!'

# Chapter 11

As Lady walked away from the prison, she wondered if she had ever really known Charlie Ackers, or for that matter, Bruce Tyler. Growing up seemed a long time ago and her life had changed so much, the reality of days gone by were hard to capture.

Her thoughts ambled back in time and she found herself seated in the little restaurant in the center of town. A few phone calls had located Charlie and he agreed to meet her for lunch. So much had changed in her life, She questioned if there would be any topics for conversation. Lady had moved into the big city, found some really close friends, found a job, joined a Church, and    settled into a more pleasant life style than ever before in her life. Sill she could not totally forget her past and she knew deep in her heart she had lost at least one, and maybe two, real friends. And maybe God had lost a couple too. And they might even need her help.

Charlie entered the door and quickly spotted the beautiful lady of the  past! He hurried to her table as if she might disappear if he were late.

"Hello Lady. It's so good to see you."

"It's good to see you too Charlie."

Not a specifically unique greeting in either direction; however, both knew how great at was to see the other again.

"Lady, you look wonderful. I just have to say it cause it's true."

"Charlie, you always make me feel so good. How have you been?"

"I guess I've been about the same as always. Haven't gotten very far from the 'tree'. How about you ?"

"Well I guess things have changed a lot for me, but it feels good to be back in the ole home town. And to see you, I might add."

The two continued to exchange greetings and were finally interrupted by the waiter. After ordering they settled into conversation of the past. It became evident that although they had been apart for quite a while, and that Lady had made some significant changes in her life, they were still attracted to each other. Of course their attractions were based on a much different basis than in previous years, at least from Lady's viewpoint.

Their visit went well and finally it was time for Lady to depart. Charlie did not want her to leave, as usual.

"I wish you could stick around for awhile."

"Me too, Charlie, but I must go. We'll get together again soon, now that I know where you are. Don't worry. I've got some real important information for you, some I should have given you long ago."

As Lady ended her thought process, she became aware, once again, that she, and most likely Charlie too, realized how much their friendship meant in their lives. Charlie admitted to himself that these visits meant a lot. 'And what if they won't let me have visitors on the Row?'

Charlie also thought about what else Lady might want to talk about. It was very obvious that over time Lady had changed, in more ways than just social life. She now was a woman, but much more than just special to him. He really didn't know what he was thinking about, but even the thought of being special to God entered his mind.

'She keeps bringing up her God and my need for him. Maybe she knows something I don't know.' Charlie realized, finally, that Lady was not just putting on a show. She had something real to give him and he must listen to her. But, listening was hard when all your thoughts were centered on Death Row!

# Chapter 12

Days in a depressing prison all seemed to run together. Likely, it was this way in all prisons. The layout was basic with no frills. A cell for sleeping and 'leisure' time. A large mess hall where food was served, but always under the careful watch of guards. And a seat in the open area for visitors. A huge wire screen separated the visitor and the victim. It was difficult to separate an assessment of how good or how bad the facilities were, because of the verdict continually hanging over a person's head.

As time passed, however, and the trend of 'social' visits increased, it seemed that maybe all days weren't the same. He could not believe he actually thought about a visit now and then. But he understood all visits were not created equal.

Charlie's daily routine was interrupted once again as he was informed that Bruce Tyler was arriving and he should move to his appointed place behind the screen.

"See Charlie, I told you old Bruce would be back. I really need to talk to you. We need to straighten some things out. Hey, look what I brought you."

At that point, the guard walked up to Charlie and handed him a package. As Charlie opened it, he began to smell the sauce from some down home bar b-q. He realized he was very lucky that the guard hadn't disappeared with his prize.

"I had to pull a string or two to get that in here."

"I can't enjoy this until I understand where you are coming from. Straighten out what things? My life is about as straight as it's going to get. My path only leads in one direction."

"You know what I'm talking about, Charlie." Bruce lowered his voice and whispered, "You know we botched that caper and you feel I should be where you are."

Charlie looked at his so-called friend and, almost rising from his seat, he said, "If I was on that side of the screen, it would offer me a ray of hope to unravel some of the issues. But wishing on my part ain't going to make it happen and nothing is going to change."

"Lighten up Charlie! I would like to help you. But you got to cut me some slack. Nobody is more disturbed than me that you're in here."

"Wanna bet! I know one that is."

"Things just didn't work out like we planned. Sometimes that happens. Everything went so fast. I didn't count on things getting so messed up."

"I counted on doing a favor for a friend and making a buck. And I didn't count on getting in trouble, and certainly not getting someone killed. I obviously didn't count far enough-or fast enough. I just wish I could remember the details."

"Maybe it's better you don't. But, you know, I wish you could fill me in on a couple of things. It would help me a lot."

"As if you needed help! But I would, if only I could remember. You do understand, however, that we can't just sit here in broad daylight and review the whole nine yards."

"I understand Charlie. You're right. We do have to be careful. But a few details won't hurt, like remembering we had two bags. But what happened to the one you were carrying?"

"I don't remember two bags. Are you sure?"

"Sure, I'm sure. Come on Charlie, don't hold out on me."

"It won't clear up. It just won't clear up."

"I've got to go for now. The guard is coming. I'll be back. Try to remember. It might help me. It might even help your case. See ya, Charlie."

Bruce's comments were causing Charlie to recapture events of the past and intertwine them into the present. Going back to his encounter with Bruce that led to participation in the Finance Office caper, about all he could remember was the invitation from Bruce to help an old friend out who had been wronged in a business deal. He had finally accepted, more from events of earlier days, but nevertheless, he had signed on for what now seemed to be beyond his reach in explanation.

Trying to reach even further back into time, Charlie seemed to bring that past into better focus. Charlie remembered many days of friendship with Bruce, starting in school and on into various jobs in the small town where they were raised. Sure, Bruce dropped out of school first, but Charlie was not far behind. The lack of money in their families and their trouble with finding time to study made school a very low second choice for their daily activity. They had one of those strange relationships where their interests were often far apart, but their actions brought them close together. Charlie had to admit that even thought they were often miles apart in motive, they hung together, almost like blood brothers.

One such experience popped into Charlie's mind. Bruce spent a great deal of time trying to increase his financial status. It sort of matched his demeanor. Most of the time these opportunities fell on dry soil with no gain. One night, however, Charlie discovered Bruce on a lonely downtown street attempting to get inside a merchandize store, with no apparent reason to be there. "What are you up to, Bruce?"

"Keep it low. I'm on to something."

"Bet you money, it's something crooked."

"Just keep quiet. There's some loose money lying around from this afternoon and I plan to have a little of it."

"Bruce, you can't keep on trying to take other people's money."

"I can, as long as I don't get caught. Why don't you help me?"

"I can't help you. Just forget it this time and let's go down to 'The Trough'."

"No chance. This is too easy."

"Bruce, if you don't get out of here, I'm going to turn you in."

"You wouldn't do that!"

"Well, I might."

"No you wouldn't"

"I guess you're right. I don't want to get you in trouble, but this has got to stop."

"It will. Believe me, it will."


Charlie found himself back in his cell wondering, for a moment, if this night might have been the beginning of his end. Things were sketchy in his mind, but it just might have been.

Thinking about the end, gave Charlie another thought to ponder. While, in all honesty it wasn't as important as his life, he did have some concern over losing Bruce. Even with all the issues, Bruce was still his connection back to birth. Even after they both became adults, using the term loosely, they hung out together for a while. Then he didn't see Bruce much for a long period. And then, out of the blue, Bruce appeared again, shortly before their adventure into stupidity.

Charlie was excited to see him again, and, he thought Bruce was equality excited. In retrospect, he now wondered if Bruce's motives were more pointed toward whatever plan he had conjured up for the Finance Office, and much less in reviewing an old friendship. Again, he couldn't blame Bruce for his fear of what might happen if he got involved in this case. Just another missing piece of a long winding puzzle that lay before him!

# Chapter 13

Once again Bruce excited the Prison quickly and seemed to take faster steps than usual. Maybe the thoughts of possibly being a participant, like  Charlie, caused him to become a little nervous. In any event, he stepped on the gas and left the scene as fast as possible.

As he drove back toward home, he passed through areas of his early life. He could not help but reflect on former times. Like Charlie, and Lady, Bruce was also tied to the past and he tried in earnest to shake it. There was  something about friendships and contacts in childhood. however, that did not  easily pass away.

Bruce drove past Smokey's Market and the past life surfaced. He too,  was overwhelmed with memories.

"Charlie, I need some help with these math problems. Can you help  me?"

"I'll try. Let's go down to the corner restaurant and sit a spell. Maybe  we can learn something."

"I'm gonna fail if I don't catch up with my homework."

"Well, we can't let that happen. Maybe I can help." He realized that Bruce must have help.

And so the two occupied a booth for several hours and poured over the  books, so to speak. Charlie was at a loss as to how to get him out of trouble.  Finally Bruce became aware of the same situation..

"Look Charlie, you've just got to let me copy some of your work. Otherwise I won't make it."

"You want me to just let you take my work to class?"

"I don't know any other answer."

"I'm concerned about your math grade, but can I just give you my  homework?"

"It won't hurt my feelings."

"What of the teacher finds out?"

"She won't find out. I promise."

And so, once again, Charlie's good heart rescued Bruce from trouble and, of course, the rest of the story is obvious. The next day, Charlie was  called in and he got the short end of the stick.

Coming back to reality, Bruce chuckled as he thought about poor Charlie. And then for only a moment, he felt sorry for him. But at the time, he had no time to waste pity on Charlie. He needed all the pity there was lying around. He needed the missing money and Charlie was his only link. Solving Death Row would have to wait so far as Bruce was concerned. He needed Charlie's help, once more!

Although it was never revealed to Bruce, this episode was likely the beginning of the end for Charlie's school days. Somehow, e lost confidence  in his school work and, to some degree, the confidence of his teachers.

"Charlie, it was not a very smart move on your part to just turn over your homework to Bruce." The teacher was very blunt and went straight to the point.

"I'm sorry, Miss Abbott. I just knew he needed some help."

"That's what your teachers are for. We can help Bruce."

" I said I'm sorry. What else can I do?"

"Well this isn't the first time that you've made a move in the wrong direction. Do you think you can straighten yourself out?"

Charlie left the school that day feeling very low. He didn't have to be told that he let Bruce get him into scrapes all the time. What was a friend supposed to do? Just let him die!

And the rest of the school story is pretty much history. Slowly Charlie lost interest, his grades went down, and school became a burden. "What does a dumb guy like me need from school anyway? I'll jus hang it up."

# Chapter 14

Although Charlie had no visitors for a few days, he could not turn loose of the events of the past week or so. What had he done and why could he not remember? Time continued to drag on as the daily chores of the prison came and went. *Maybe I just need to let it go for awhile.* But deep down inside Charlie knew that was unlikely and sooner, or later, another visitor would appear. Also deep down, Charlie felt something inside him changing.

The next morning as Chaplain Barney Howard approached the prison cage, Charlie remembered his pledge and prediction. *Well, maybe this is what he needed.*

"Good morning, again, Charlie. As usual, it's good to see you."

"Thanks for coming, Chaplain. Welcome to my home. I guess this is the first time you've heard those words from me."

"Well, yes it is, but I go to a lot of homes, uninvited, and likely unwanted. I guess you could say, it goes with the territory."

"Anyway, I'm glad you're here. I need to talk and clear up some of this blur. And you're what I've got. My mind is really messed up."

"What do you mean?"

"I can't sleep at night. I walk the floor. I'm confused. I'm scared. I even think about God occasionally, but usually in the wrong sense. I mean, you tell me God loves me, even in my situation. However I would say, He's about to get His just rewards."

"Your theology is a little bit out of skew there Charlie. God's not out to get you, at least not in the sense you mean. He wants you all right, but in a totally different way."

"Anyway, I need some relief! Can you help me?"

"I'd say you need relief in two directions."

"In two directions?"

"You need God's relief from your life long burdens, and they are numerous. You also need some personal relief from current trouble. I believe you are agonizing over the events that got you in here. And I don't mean the obvious."

"Well, tell me the unobvious then."

"I believe you are beginning to realize that you don't belong in here, at least not headed to Death Row. You committed a crime, or were associated with one. The new facts of your case, however, are beginning to cast a lot of doubt on the magnitude of your guilt."

"Who have you been talking to? How can they know more than I do?"

"Charlie, you're going to have to trust me on this one. And trust God. I know that's a hard one right now. I have an appointment this afternoon, but I'll be back as soon as possible. I don't want to get your hopes up too high, because the case on the books is solid against you. In all fairness, though, there may be information that just never made it to the books. We've got to move on though, because it looks like you may be moving to Death Row soon."

"How do you know that? My lawyer hasn't mentioned it. And why are you so involved?"

"That's a hard one to answer, Charlie. I'm not an expert, but your comments, and maybe God's direction, caused me to ponder your situation. You just don't fit the picture. Of course I don't know exactly what the picture looks like, but I don't think I could have left this situation without some inquiry. Some of my conversations with the legal folks indicates that appeal is not working and the move may be imminent. Your lawyer probably is trying to save you from bad news."

"That's pretty deep, Chaplain. But I'm grateful. You know I kid and gripe a lot, but most of it is a way to live with my situation. I have to admit I am grateful to you for your interest in me. I also have to admit, based on my previous life, this place isn't as bad as I make it out to be. Obviously, that's not a very positive statement, just one of fact."

"Charlie, I appreciate your comments."

"How can the world we grew up in be so different?

"Maybe it wasn't, Charlie. Maybe we have just gone in different directions."

"Well, your world seems a long way from mine, but maybe mine is changing a little. I will admit that my heart seems to be changing."

"That's great news, Charlie. We don't want to let the current troubles hanging over your head keep you from an even more important decision you need to make. You know I haven't presented a Bible story to you in several days and I have a good one. Fits you in some sense."

"A Bible story fits me?"

"Well you know what I mean. Another example for you to think about."

"Well bring it on."

"Did you ever here of Paul in the Bible?"

"Can't say that I have, but my Bible reading has not been very deep."

"Paul initially used the name of Saul. He persecuted Christians. God spoke to him one day and his life changed. He then spent a lot of time moving around the country spreading the Word of God and talking about Jesus, God's Son. And after all his good work, he wound up in Prison. You can identify with that."

"I haven't done much good work, but I can identify with the prison part."

"Did Paul let that stop him from doing his work. Absolutely not. He kept right on sending out the message. Once he was even stoned, but he survived. So you see, you need to meet God, no matter what your real crime or real verdict is. And there is plenty of good work to do, even in a prison. Let me go now and I'll be back soon.

Charlie sat in the chair, more puzzled than ever. 'What did the Chaplain know? What has he got to gain? Why would God be involved in this mess? How could I meet God in Prison? How could I work for him in Prison?' He felt like he was about to lose it all. But then, hadn't he already done that? Maybe it's time to pick up the pieces. Maybe it's time to answer the question of why I'm headed to Death Row.

# Chapter 15

After the Chaplain's visit, Charlie sat in his cell and thought about the past. He wondered, as usual, why his memory of the events of his problem were so hidden in his mind. Today he felt different. Today he thought maybe the past could be revisited.

Charlie had visited many of his earlier episodes with Bruce. The tie between them was difficult to explain. Many times they got into trouble by accident. Many times it was a planned venture. 'Why did I keep being pulled into Bruce's troubles?'

Often Charlie would say to himself, 'I can't be involved in any more of this. One day, it's going to fall apart.' And bang, it did! In retrospect, he finally admitted to himself that his fear of losing Bruce as a friend, using the term loosely, was often greater than his desire to stay out of trouble. Many times he would avoid the issues and then, at the last minute, would fold up and do Bruce's bidding.

One such occasion was the day of the beginning of the end. Bruce had laid out the big plan for getting into the Finance building. In all honesty, Charlie actually thought Bruce was trying to resolve a big mistake that had cost him some bucks. 'Am I trying to deceive myself or did I actually believe Bruce was almost on the level on this one?' Which ever way it was, Bruce had yielded to the temptation. While not very clear in his mind, Charlie did remember coming to the building. Maybe he even remembered entering the place. Beyond that, it was a dead end street.

The only bright spot was that it appeared the Chaplain was in his corner and was desperately trying to help him. It suddenly dawned on him that Barney's help might go beyond the trial. It might be help for his soul. And the good Lord knew he needed that help. 'Could it be possible that I might get to a point where my soul was more important than my body? What am I saying? I've been hearing too much spiritual talk. I don't speak this language. But I might learn it. Who knows?'

How would any one help him if he, himself, couldn't even remember the real facts? God might look down on him in pity, but that isn't going to help solve this mystery. 'I can't give up, though. I just can't'.

The more he thought about the situation, the more involved God seemed to be. What caused this to happen? 'God doesn't throw you in prison just to help you straighten out your life. Or dies he? Well not really, but since I'm here, maybe it's time I listen to God a little. What a change for me!'

# Chapter 16

Later that afternoon Barney met with personnel in the DA's office once again to put some of the court information into his puzzle. The DA had reluctantly agreed to release the records the first time, but did so with no promise of any follow-up activity.

As usual, the facts presented in the prosecutor's case were easier to assimilate than the myriad of information the defense normally spins together. Barney had finally gathered enough data to see where the missing links were. Basically they all fell at Bruce's feet. Unfortunately, however, no one at the trial knew there was a Bruce.

"Based on your comments and questions, I assume you believe Charlie Ackers is innocent of the charges placed against him." The DA moved directly to the point, even though he had no idea where the Chaplain was heading.

"I am not sure what Charlie is guilty of, but I feel there is a strong possibility that someone else is involved also."

"Well, as you were told by the Judge, as far as this case is concerned, there is no other party."

"I understand. That is the troubling part of this whole affair."

Barney invited Lady Martin to come to his office the next morning so that he might fill her in on the latest details. Lady's nerves were at fever pitch as she moved around the office. Barney was getting nowhere with his speech. "Lady, wouldn't you like to sit down? You make me nervous. It's hard to hit a moving target."

"I'm too nervous to sit. I need to keep moving. I need to use up some of my energy to keep my temper in check."

"I know what you mean. After unraveling some of these puzzles, I could join you, but it isn't in keeping with my profession."

"So you think the facts were stacked against Charlie?"

"Yes, I do. The problem is, I'm not sure there is anything we can do about it. It's gone so far."

"How did it get this far without all the facts? Don't answer that. I know how."

"You're right, Lady, there was one important participant missing at the trial. And unless we get him involved, there will be no reversal of the verdict."

"Well, let's get him involved. Do it! A man's life is on the line here. And not just any man, a special friend of mine. And I'm afraid he isn't ready to meet God, just yet."

"I understand where you are coming from and I agree with you. There's only one small problem."

"And that is..."

"The missing participant appears to be Bruce! And there is no way to get him involved except for Bruce to get himself involved. The court can't touch him. I have that straight from the Judge. Bruce does not exist at this point. Based on the data, if there was a missing person, legally it could be anyone."

"Well surely Bruce will come forward if he knows he can help."

"Would you? Oh, I'm sorry, I just couldn't resist the temptation. Only to make a point! Of course you would. But will Bruce? I doubt it. For Bruce to come forward would mean major involvement. And worse than that, most likely major jail involvement. And possibly even Death Row involvement."

"What! You've got to be kidding."

"I wish I were!"

"You apparently have information you haven't shared with me."

"Well, not intentionally. I gave you the big picture before. You see, as best as I have been able to put this together with the Police records, a private investigator, the DA, Charlie's comments, and a little conjecture on my part, there is a missing person involved and it has to be Bruce. Nobody knows who Bruce is and most aren't interested in finding out because they have a convicted individual ready for Death Row. Charlie was partially a victim of the crime, as well as a participant. Granted he should never have been at the scene. He made a mistake, but his biggest mistake was getting involved with Bruce Tyler, the real culprit."

"Please tell me all the facts. This is unreal."

"Bruce apparently got Charlie involved for a minor role, maybe agreeing to drive the car for what Charlie thought was a "little" crime, and he did it as a friend. Charlie wasn't naive, but he never explored the magnitude of what Bruce had in mind. It never occurred to him, cause he thought he knew Bruce."

"So did I." Lady felt great remorse as she accepted the truth.

"How wrong you both were! Based on the facts I have been able to put together, Charlie was supposed to wait in the car for an agreed to time and then enter the office of the Chief Financial Officer. Charlie knew he would possibly be involved in some unfriendly activity. Apparently, it was planned that Charlie would arrive just in time to be a proxy for a tough guy with some 'if you don't do what I want, it's going to be rough' talk."

"What happened then?"

"Well, the situation must have gotten hot quicker than Bruce anticipated. Or Charlie was much later than he was supposed to be. In any event, Bruce did the heavy talking and started to force the opening of the safe. The CFO likely objected and was struck somehow. The safe was set to blow. The explosion must have startled a guard who was close by. Bruce had only begun to fill the first bag when he realized he had to exit. In his haste, he dropped the bag. It was recovered at the investigation. The second bag, to be filled by Charlie, was also left behind. Then Charlie enters and the world turns up side down."

Lady could hardly believe all she was hearing. "How could Charlie have been so naive about this whole situation? Good ole Charlie, always a sucker for Bruce's tactics."

Barney continued, "Incorrectly, there was a second explosion just as Charlie entered the room and it knocked him unconscious and killed the CFO, who must have moved closer to the safe. Charlie wakes up stunned before the guard enters. The guard then finds a killer, a corpse, and a bag.

"So the plan went wrong and Charlie got caught in the middle."

"That's right. And they both were losers. Charlie got arrested for murder and Bruce lost the money he broke into the building for. And now you know why Bruce has finally made the effort to renew an old 'friendship'. "

"He thinks Charlie knows where the money is." Lady paused a moment and then uttered these words softly. "Does he?"

"I don't think so. Anyway, it isn't going to do him any good on the road he's on. Otherwise, I believe he would have told someone, someone like you."

"Tell me the rest. What was missing from the trial?"

"I will, but we have to move fast. Another guard saw an unidentified person in the building, but could not identify him or associate him with the murder. Also, after the fact, the guard that testified felt like Charlie's condition may have been more serious than stated at the trial and now wasn't sure but that he might also have been a victim of the explosion. Of course Charlie could have set off both the explosions, but the timing wasn't exactly right."

"And to make matters even worse, we have to override a trial that has pronounced him guilty. And, based on my own personal investigation of criminal trials through the media, radio, and TV, this case is a classic example of finding the 'likely not- guilty party', 'guilty'. What a shame!"

"That's almost too much information to take in at one time. And so surprising!"

"Lady, I need a big favor from you. You've known Bruce and Charlie a long time. If anyone can talk Bruce into helping with this, you are the one. Will you give it a try?"

"This is a challenge that I may not be able to pull off. You know how guys are. But I'll give it a try."

"That's great! Also, you need to know that Charlie may be realizing his need for God. Sometimes it takes a thunderbolt for that to happen."

"Well, he certainly has had the thunderbolt! And he is very lucky to have encountered a person like you."

"I believe I have had some great help from the Lord himself. And your friendship and caring for Charlie haven't hurt this situation either.

As Lady walked toward her car, she realized how important her assignment was. Without Bruce in the plan, Charlie did not have a chance. The more she thought about it, the more nervous she became. At first the possibilities for Charlie were somewhat open, but now the options were very few, maybe only one. 'I can't drop this ball. If I fail, Death Row is just around the corner.'

# Chapter 17

Lady wasted no time in locating Bruce and inviting him to lunch at his favorite corner restaurant. Not the same as it was a hundred years ago, but nevertheless, a spot that brought back many memories. They were seated and ordered, and then Lady dropped the bombshell.

"You want me to do what?" Bruce waved his arms and almost fell out of the chair. "Are you crazy?"

"I want you to do Charlie a big favor. We go back a long way Bruce. He was our friend. He's in trouble for his life. He needs you."

"You want me to go to the police! You want me to give myself up! Are you nuts? Do you know what they would do to me? They would crucify me!"

"Bruce, it's the right thing to do. You have to. How many times along the way did Charlie rescue you from trouble? Have you forgotten his role in your life?"

"Lady, get real! You are asking the impossible. Charlie is guilty of a crime. If I get involved, it won't help him, I'll just get myself in trouble too."

"Would you agree to sit down with Charlie and me and talk about this?"

"Well, I'm not crazy about the idea. I need to think about it."

"Bruce, you've got to help."

"Get off my back and let me have some time."

"We don't have any time. Charlie's time is getting short."

"What good is a sit down?"

"We don't know, but it might help. Please Bruce."

Bruce knew Lady was not going to go down easy. He could cut and run, but she would just come after him. Maybe it wouldn't hurt. So what? Charlie can't hurt me now. "OK, I'll do it, but it will be short and I ain't making any promises."

As the pair parted the restaurant, Bruce's mind ran a tape of memories of the crime so fast it made him dizzy. What was he getting into? Why did he agree to do this? It might be a lose, lose situation.

He knew if he gave this subject too much thought, it would get harder and harder to escape. But this was ridiculous. He would go down the drain and Charlie might or might not be helped. He knew it would be easy to think more about himself than someone else, but then he was used to this position. "What have I gotten myself into?"

As the pair parted the restaurant, Lady's mind quickly laid out a plan. She had to get the Chaplain to be present at the talk and she had to keep Bruce in tow until something could be worked out. What a chore!

She knew that she had placed Bruce in a very bad situation. What he said was true. Nothing might help Charlie and anything would drown Bruce. She eased back in her car seat and took a deep breath. We'll just have to move forward and see what happens.

Lady began to plan the tactics for the crucial meeting before her. It had been a long time since the three of them had gathered together for anything. And she knew when the Chaplain appeared Bruce would smell a rat and who could know what his reaction would be. Well, we have to meet, so full speed ahead!

# Chapter 18

The next morning Lady and Bruce entered the prison area and sat down across from Charlie. Charlie had not been read into the situation, but he could sense some uneasiness as he watched Bruce and Lady arrive. In a few minutes Chaplain Barney entered the room. Neither Bruce, nor Charlie, expected this entrance.

"I'm sorry I'm late."

Bruce leaned over and whispered to Lady, "You didn't tell me you invited the Parson."

Lady returned the whisper, "I thought it would be a good idea."

"This is an interesting meeting. Chaplain, except for you, this is like a family reunion." While Charlie was not totally in outer space, he really did not grasp the total significance of the group's visit.

The Chaplain sat down and the room became quiet. "Charlie, we're here because we have some new information about your case. I told you I would be back soon. I have received permission from the State Prison to have this meeting. And we have been guaranteed privacy."

"Bruce, where do you fit in all this? My mind is so confused, I can't sort it out." Again, Charlie appeared to have no concept of the magnitude of Bruce's involvement.

At this point Barney decided to take control of the session. He had the information and in some sense, he was the person in charge here.

"Bruce, let me catch us up to speed. Then you can help. Here's what we think we know. Our new information indicates that someone entered the finance building prior to Charlie's entrance. An argument or fight ensued and a safe was blown. Apparently, the intruder spotted another guard and fled from the scene to somewhere else in the building. It appears that Charlie had been waiting outside. At some point Charlie went inside. A great big mistake! But Charlie chose to play the game. He just didn't count the cost.

Upon entering the building, Charlie apparently found the room where the safe was located. Just as he entered there was a violent explosion. Unknown to Charlie, this was a second explosion, caused by a faulty detonator. He was unconscious for some minutes. When he awoke and his head cleared, what he discovered was a blown safe, a dead CFO, and a guard hovering over him. The rest of the story is in the record."

Bruce, and Charlie, sat in disbelief as the Chaplain unfolded the story. While both men were listening from totally different perspectives, neither of them actually saw the killing. Lady spoke up to add the finishing touch.

"And Bruce, you were the other person in the building related to the break-in. And no one saw you. An unlikely scenario, but nevertheless, a true one."

Charlie's face turned pale. "You are telling me that the explosion happened as I entered the room, and everything there had already happened? I find it hard to believe this story." While it removed much of the fog from his mind, it introduced Bruce as the main culprit, a totally new wrinkle, and one disappointing to Charlie.

"That's right, Charlie", said Barney.

"Bruce? You were robbing this building? And a person was killed. I don't think I can comprehend all this at one time. Not the Bruce I knew."

"And Bruce, you are the key to straighten this out. This is your chance to turn your life around." Lady hit him where it hurt, but Bruce was not on the same page at the moment.

"Wait a minute!" Bruce jumped to his feet. "Let's get this straight. Charlie knew I was in the building. He drove me there. And I wasn't even in the room when the CFO was killed. I never saw it. The past is the past. What's done is done. Charlie, I can't help you even if I told everything. This case has been settled. And the only change would be my undoing. What do you people want? Flesh and blood. Let's get serious!"

Barney chimed in at this point. "We are serious, Bruce. You know what really happened that night. You are the only one who can step up and do the right thing, save an innocent man, and a friend. This is your call. What will it be?"

"Don't put a guilt trip on me!

"I don't mean to do that. What I mean to do is to give you something to think and pray about. I have shared Bible stories with Charlie about persons who did bad things and who did good things and who wound up in prison. It did not ruin their lives. In many cases it changed their lives. People like John the Baptist, Jesus' Apostles, and many others. Some situations ended good and some ended humanly bad, but God was always there to help the people deal with their issues. We are all called on to be God's helpers. "

"I can't help Charlie here. It would ruin my life. Charlie's fate is fixed, no matter what I do. Get off my back. I can't take any more of this. I'm out of here!"

Bruce raced out of the room and out into the free world. The day was warm, sunny, and pleasant. He tried not to think about what happened. He had decisions to make and some of them could be costly.

Pushing the events of the meeting out of sight became impossible. 'How in the world did I ever get myself into this?' I was the luckiest guy in the world when I wasn't caught at the scene. Now I've let it get screwed up. Will I ever learn?

# Chapter 19

Getting back into his normal routine, Bruce soon realized that no matter what job he encountered, wrestling with his decisions was going to be sitting right there in the middle of the pile. And no matter which approach he took to solve his dilemma, or Charlie's, he would be faced with choices unbearable and unacceptable at this point. 'I think I'm going crazy!'

Bruce revisited his childhood often during the next few days . Why couldn't life be simple like it was in those days? Poor as job's turkey, yet living on easy street, so to speak. Maybe it was just another type of worry, one that didn't keep you awake at night.

While Charlie often growled at Bruce about some of his ideas and plans, Bruce realized that seldom did he, himself, ever think about the consequences. That kind of thinking ruined the whole plan. Or did it? Maybe I was a little off in my judgment in those days. Maybe that's why I'm having so much trouble now. I've never been here before!

Bruce sat in his room in the dark and began to reflect on stories from the past. While many of their escapades were rather simple and caused no real problems, a few got out of hand. Even Bruce had to admit that. At least now he did. At the time it went right over his head.

"Charlie, have you noticed the way Smokey leaves his cash drawer sort of open, occasionally?"

"Well, not really. I guess that's a part of the business I never get into."

"Well maybe it's time we did, get into."

"What do you mean?"

"We've played games around Smokey from time to time, but we've really never gone for the prize with him. Maybe it's time"

"What on earth are you thinking about now?"

"Charlie, you get too disturbed. I'm just thinking about how sweet it would be to get a few dollars out of that drawer and have no one know it was us."

"Bruce, you are nuts. That's stealing."

"We've had a few bucks out of there. Does stealing have a size?"

"I'm not sure what you have on your mind, but I do not want to get in trouble."

"I believe I've heard that sour note before."

"Maybe so, Bruce. Can't we have a little fun without going over the hill?"

"Sure we can!"

Bruce chuckled to himself as he thought about how easy it was to get ole Charlie all tied up and confused. He had to admit he had pulled this trick on Charlie many times and this episode was no exception.

The two worked out a plan. Charlie thinking that he was a small participant and never realizing that Bruce was leading him into anything bad. How many times? Bruce chuckled again as he thought about the results. Then suddenly he realized his treatment of Charlie in that caper tied directly into the current events. Why had he never thought of this before? Now he was sorry he had visited this experience because it struck him right in the heart. 'I never meant to get Charlie in trouble.'

The following days became long and hard. Bruce became weary as time passed. One day he was on Plan a, and then, here he was on Plan b. 'What can I do to get out of this mess?'

# Chapter 20

The meeting had ended abruptly. No one expected an instant cure, but Bruce's exit left the group in doubt. Would he come back? Would he think about what he had done? Could he do this to a friend? The three stood in silence. Finally Charlie broke the silence.

"I'm in a state of shock. I can't believe what I've heard. I trusted a person I thought was a friend, a person I really didn't know. What a fool I was!"

Lady moved as close to Charlie as possible. A tear came to her eye. "We tried Charlie, we really did. I don't understand why the law can't correct this mistake."

"This is a tough blow, Charlie", Barney chimed in. "However, we don't know what Bruce will do. He may or may not come around. Looking back, it might have been better to leave things just as they were. But he has a chance to reverse his life, spiritually, and probably has never thought about it."

"He's right Charlie", Lady added. "We've only made things worse for you. As much as I want to, I can't believe that Bruce will see the light. And in any event you don't have much time."

Charlie listened to his real friends digest the events and possible reactions. Then he interrupted the group. "Wait a minute! Let's think about this. My life has been a shambles. I made a gross error. My whole life has been a gross error. I never believed Bruce was going to steal all that money. I thought he was going in there to get some money the company had beaten him out of. Say, now I know why he was so interested in that bag. I was stupid to believe him. I was stupid to be there. I bet Bruce will never know that the second bag was blown to bits... But, you guys have cleared up all this fuzziness. More important to me, you have cared about me. You don't know how much that means."

As Charlie digested words he was hearing from his two primary mentors, he felt a closeness to them that was different. It replaced a more sensual and hurt feeling toward Lady, even though his total feelings for her would likely never change. It created a new feeling toward Barney. Most of Charlie's distance from Barney resulted from his dual assignment. On the one hand he was Charlie's religious mentor and in the past Charlie had little need for that. On the other hand Barney was employed by an organization that would eventually put him in the ground if things did not change. "But now, how could I have hard feelings for these people?"

"Charlie, we do care about you." Once again Lady looked at Charlie with a memory from the past.

"And we care about your soul too. This isn't a good place for someone to be who is at odds with the good Lord." The Chaplain looked Charlie in the eye as he talked. He knew Charlie was touched and, in fact, changed.

"You're right, Chaplain. And I'm working on that. God has placed two very special people in my life and I've got to sort out what God has in store for someone with as little longevity as I have."

Charlie moved as close to the screen as he could get. He continued, "You know, all this thinking I've been doing, maybe it will pay off. Even though I didn't have all the facts right, I do know that all the prisoners in the world aren't behind bars. You've shared your Bible stories with me. And everywhere a person is working for God, there are a lot of people, like me, hurting, either in or out of the prison."

"You've come a long way from Winter's Market, Charlie." Even though she was there as a missionary, Lady knew that her memories from the past were a strong tool in her prayers for Charlie.

"Lady's right, Charlie, and most of us don't have all the facts right. God's word, the real facts, is available for us all, but many of us choose to ignore it. I believe, though, that you're on the right track."

Charlie looked at his two friends. Two friends that cared enough about him to be here. As bad as things were, he knew he was blessed. He rose from his seat and uttered a profound statement.

"Although I'm not happy about my physical situation, or for that matter, Bruce's, let me finally tell the whole truth. Bruce may or may not come to my rescue. Time is important, but for whom? I've got a lot more time, at the moment, than he does. Regardless of the outcome, think about it. WHO IS ON THEIR WAY TO DEATH ROW HERE ANYWAY? CHARLIE OR BRUCE?

Maybe I'm supposed to give my life to save Bruce. Otherwise, why I am headed to my Death Row is of little consequence at this point."

# THE END

# OR

# THE BEGINNING!

The opportunity
to become the person
that you were meant to be
is always just a decision away.

# EPILOG

From a human standpoint, the preceding events led to a major crossroad. Bruce Tyler might take the right turn to help a friend. He might repent of his wrongdoing and turn his life around. Charlie Ackers might be able to have a second trial and he might be acquitted. On the other hand, Bruce Tyler might take a left turn and drive on, for a while at least. After all, he controlled the crossing and made the choices for both men.

From a spiritual standpoint, the preceding events led to a major intersection. Even though Charlie Ackers was on the road to human death, he had claimed a seat on the road to heaven. At the moment, Bruce Tyler was dealing with his conscience, if he had one, and was definitely on the main road to everlasting death. He might change his course along the way; however, as stated above, he controlled his own choice. He did not, however, control the spiritual choice of Charlie Ackers. Charlie chose to make, and cross, the major intersection. His choice was sealed.

**THE END**

**OR**

**THE BEGINNING!**

# EPILOGUE II

Time passed and each day Charlie became more nervous about his possible Death Row situation, but more stable in his belief in God and His blessings. On the other side of the picture, Bruce went back to his less than profitable job at the local car repair shop. Like it or not, he had heard the words of his long time 'friend' and it became difficult to hide them from his attention. He tried a few of his old tricks, but nothing seemed to break the feelings he had. Finally, he decided that he would pay Charlie another visit. He hoped he had not waited too long!

"Hi Charlie. Thanks for seeing me again."

"I could hardly deny you a visit."

"Don't get me wrong. I know you want me here, but you want my words, not my person."

"Bruce, you might be wrong. You won't believe it, but I have made my peace with my God. No one wants to die, but I am ready. I could never explain the change in my attitude and feelings now that my real future is settled."

"Charlie, I don't really understand what you are saying, but I do know that I have not been exactly without feelings about your situation. I am sorry for all this trouble. I should never have dragged you into this mess. I really didn't mean for it to end as it did. I guess I thought that I could dance into the Finance Shop and they would lie down and give up. It was foolish of me and really stupid."

"Well, you're not alone in stupidity. I should have known that throwing the dice for a few unearned bucks would never pay off."

Bruce sat quietly a few seconds. He did not know where to go next. "I'm really lost as to what to say to you. I honestly don't think there is anything I can do to help your situation, but I can't seem to get it out of my mind. What can I do?"

"That's not for me to say, Bruce. And I don't know what I would say if it was."

"Your case has been tried. The original evidence left me out. The new evidence left me out. What good would my words do by throwing myself at the Judge?"

"I don't know. If I'm going to die for the deed, what good is your input? I'm not the expert here."

"Who is the expert? Why don't you get your Preacher guy to tell us who we need."

"Bruce, do you know what you're saying?"

"Yes, I do. My life won't ever be any good any more if I just sit here and let you take it all."

"I can accept your gift, but I won't have any peace about it unless you let God into your life."

"Maybe the Preach can help me with that too."

"That would be terrific, Bruce! Just terrific."

Both men sat in a state of excitement and shock! Charlie could not believe that Bruce would make such a sacrifice for him, but felt a closeness never before felt. 'Would I do what Bruce is doing if we were swapped in our issues?', Charlie muttered to himself.

Bruce gathered his thoughts and wondered how he made it to this point in his life. 'Why am I taking this chance?', he thought. 'What has happened to me?'

The longer he thought, the more mixed up the two choices became. While filled with the thoughts that Charlie needed his help, and that maybe, Bruce needed God, the great picture of

Death Row kept blurring the scene. He realized things had to move fast, before he backed out and fled.

# EPILOGUE III

$F$inally, the two guys came back to reality. Charlie made the first sound.

"Bruce, can you fill me in on all the details you can remember. I've heard a lot of information, but I need to hear some from you. Just for my sanity, not necessarily to be used in a new trial."

"Well Charlie, I guess it wouldn't hurt any. I trust you, but even if you blabbed all this to the Judge, he couldn't use it."

"You can trust me Bruce. And I would like to be able to trust you."

"As you know there are parts of this story that you don't remember because you were out, and some I don't remember because I wasn't there all the time. But here is want I can tell you."

Bruce began a dialog and Charlie sat more rigid and stunned than probably ever before. Occasionally Charlie would recognize a piece of the story. Most of the time he didn't.

Ole man Harrison was CFO at the Finance Office where most of the city's major transactions were carried on. Being a small community, the business was considerably smaller than average, but nevertheless, it was business. Somehow Bruce got a piece of information that the lot next door to Smokey's Market was to be sold. The owner was a distant relative of Bruce's father and again, somehow, Bruce got enough information to set up a meeting with Mr. Harrison.

Bruce had one plan he laid out to Charlie with a perfectly legitimate reason to be meeting. He had a second plan that was about 180 degrees different. Charlie was to drive the car to the Office, wait a short time while Bruce negotiated with the CFO an agreement that Bruce could represent the family, discuss some paper work, and get a small payment for his participation.

In reality, Bruce was to meet with the CFO, spread a few tales about the sale, negotiate a price, and then force a small portion of the settlement. If he bogged down in the dispute, Charlie would eventually enter the office and Bruce would use him for a distraction while moving toward a goal of relieving the Finance Office of a few funds.

As had already been described, the plan got confused, Charlie and the CFO were involved in an explosion, and Bruce exited the building, unseen for identity.

"Well Bruce, this clears up a number of missing links, but it sure is a far cry from where I was headed in the plan. I wish I didn't know all this now, but I guess it's a little late. Truth is truth, no matter how bad. Thanks for the words."

"Well now you know. So let's get on with it!"

# EPILOGUE IV

Charlie and Bruce sat down with the Chaplain once again and laid out their story. Barney Howard likely had never encountered such a series of events in his career. He thought he was elated when Bruce agreed to talk to someone. When he found out Bruce was also agreeable to talk to God about his situation, he was ecstatic. While the most current problem was the trial, the most important problem was Bruce's relationship with God.

"Bruce, I have shared a few Bible stories with Charlie over time and I believe, he, as well as I, can help you see God's plan for you. I certainly pray that we can."

After discussion, the Chaplain agreed to talk, off the record, to the District Attorney. He did not want to promise Bruce anything because he had no idea how the DA would or could react. It was agreed by Barney that he would not divulge Bruce's name in the discussions. He did not know if the DA would accept this or not.

The Chaplain entered the Court House with great anticipation on the one hand and with great doubt on the other. After weeks of exhaustive investigation and interviews, he was convinced, not only of participation in the caper by Bruce Tyler, but also significant doubt about Charlie Acker's involvement. Communicating this unofficial and unproven information in a convincing manner to the DA would be a challenge.

"Chaplain Howard, how do you expect legal changes with the trial closed and 'hear-say' data?"

"Mr. District Attorney, I have gathered significant information, both from participants in the trial and from people familiar with the events that took place. I understand your position, but in the interest of justice, I must be heard. There is no doubt that another party was involved in this crime."

"At the best, we are treading on slippery ground here. Rules are rules!"

"I understand. First of all, I have no connection with the defendant. I have no motive to change the findings except on a good faith basis. Lastly, I have nothing personal to gain."

"Can you identify this second party?"

"Yes, but not until I have official agreement to set another trial."

"How can we make such a decision unless we have confessions from the second party?"

And so the discussions continued. Finally, it was concluded that any effort to create a new trial with a new witness would likely end up either with no change in the sentence for Charlie or the same plus an unknown period of jail time for Bruce. The Chaplain was not happy with this conclusion. The DA made it clear once again, as the Judge had laid it out before; there would be no more discussions without a new named witness.

Barney, Charlie, and Bruce met once again and after some discussion time, looked at each other in anguish. "What should we do?", asked Barney.

"There is only one thing to do. We've got to give the DA my name and have a sit down with the four of us." Bruce made it very clear that this was the course of action necessary.

The next meeting was set and then several discussions followed. The DA was very puzzled that Bruce had entered the picture. He apparently had little concept of 'helping your fellow man'. The

Chaplain tried to expand the reasons for Bruce's involvement. It was never clear if he succeeded or not.

While the motive for a new trial was very clear to Barney, his need to sell the idea to the DA became exhausting. Even when the case had been carefully laid out and generally accepted, the DA had to deal with his own pride. After all, how often is the DA wrong? But he did acknowledge that much of the first case was more default than proven.

Finally, the DA set in motion a second trial. It was very complicated. Time had passed. The details were numerous. The original verdict was very imposing on any new findings. Much of the original testimony was conjecture rather than actual facts. Bruce's comments were perhaps the most impressive, but, as with the DA, the jury was very confused about his motive for appearance. Many days passed.

At last the jury was discharged with a goal of finding a new verdict. More time passed. Several times the jurors requested clarification on topics. On what became the final day of deliberation, the Jury sat around the table with several differing positions,

The foreman of the jury had become quite frustrated at his assignment. He needed something concrete to seal a position and bring the group together. Finally, one of the jurors rose and asked to speak.

"Mr. Foreman, we have deliberated old data and new data. From these discussions, it has become quite clear that the original findings and verdict were brought to conclusion with what appeared to be hasty and inconclusive decisions. My comments are not so much to criticize the findings, but to point out that further review and analysis has rendered those findings as speculative and quite argumentative. Granted, with the information available and presented at the time, the findings did point significantly to one individual. To paraphrase these comments, it was almost a verdict based on 'no other candidates' available."

At this point the gentleman speaking was interrupted with a comment of agreement. "You are absolutely correct. And the jury was left with no other choices and someone had to pay for the murder."

With these comments on the table, the Foreman interjected his position on the current question. "Thank you for your comments. I believe you have led us correctly to the present situation. We are now faced with a somewhat similar position as before, only this time we have two available candidates. There is no evidence to indicate any other involvement. And there is not enough evidence to conclusively reach a decision on who is more responsible for this murder, even though we have a potential victim and a signed confession. In other words, we can't prove, conclusively, that Charlie Ackers is totally innocent and that Bruce Tyler is totally guilty."

The Jury sat in silence at this point as the foreman finished his comments.

"Finally, it is my opinion, from the data presented at both trials, that this murder was not premeditated. Therefore based on all the above, I recommend that we find both parties equally guilty and recommend prison assignments rather than Death Row."

The Jury members concurred. At last they found resolution.

Back in the courtroom, the Judge made the following request. "Would the jury please present your verdict." The Judge was as uneasy at the thought of the impending news as anyone else in the courtroom. Well, excluding Charlie and Bruce. And the Chaplain was very emotional at the entire sequence of events.

"Your honor, we have two findings. First, we resend the Death Row charge from the first trial." Charlie emotions flooded his body. Bruce broke into a great sweat. Barney sat stunned. "Second, we find the two parties, Charlie Ackers and Bruce Tyler, equally guilty of the charge of unpremeditated murder. It is recommended that both men be sentenced to prison for an extended period to be determined, with no chance for parole."

While the new trial covered a long period of time, the significant change in results came down so sudden that all interested parties left the courtroom, basically stunned in silence. Charlie, along with Bruce, was immediately placed back in prison awaiting a decision on the length of the sentence. Barney Howard returned to his office with mixed emotions about the whole situation. Had he done the right thing? Did he help anybody? And Lady returned to her home, both saddened and relieved. She also had second thoughts about her contribution to the new events.

The next day Barney and Lady met to discuss what had happened. "Did we do the right thing?", she asked.

"We did the best that we could do. It was impossible to outguess the jury."

"I suppose we thought deep in our hearts that Charlie would be freed and Bruce would bear the brunt of the punishment."

"I'm sure that is where we silently thought this case would end. But before we get too low with the results, let's remember that Charlie is better off than he was, believe it or not. And Bruce deserved some punishment. And, on a somewhat lighter side, I imagine the jury is still trying to discern motive for Bruce's appearance. Sad, but true."

Lady paused for a moment, then looked the Chaplain in the eye. "You are right! Charlie, though incarcerated, can find a place to serve God and his fellow prisoners. The options are great."

"And Bruce came forward and was spared his life and can find God, even in a prison, if he chooses to. And isn't God wonderful, sparing Charlie the pain of having to spend time on Death Row!"

"And Chaplain, isn't God wonderful that Charlie did not have to die to save Bruce? Maybe we didn't do so bad after all."

"And maybe Charlie and Bruce won't do so bad either. Another one that didn't do so bad is Jesus, himself."

"Well, you're right, but what do you mean?"

"Think about this! I've talked to Charlie, and Bruce, about people and their bout with prisons and Death Row. The Bible is full of such stories and there are many others happening every day. The human Jesus was on Death Row from the day he was born to the day he died. And look at his life, his ministry, and the people he touched, including you and me, and what he accomplished."

"Chaplain, you are so right!"

And so this story continues. How does it end? Where does it end? Only the good Lord knows. But for Charlie and Bruce, it's still----------------------

# THE END

# OR

# THE BEGINNING!

# The greatest decision
# ever made
# for the prisoners
# of this world!

# EPILOGUE V

For those who always want, from a human standpoint, a totally "Happily Ever After" ending, this story has likely not filled the need. God does, however, have a message here. First of all, when people are in trouble, God can still rescue them for eternity, sometimes without a resolve of human events. And second, when people are in trouble, they still have the option to turn their back on God, in order to attempt improvement of their resolve of human events.

Another message worthy of note also relates to the severity of the possible outcomes from this story. Consider the number of opportunities people have each day to come to the aid of their friends and 'neighbors' that have no life threatening possibilities. It is something to think about, and pray about! God will open the doors. All we have to do is come in.

As Charlie pointed out to us, when the world is falling apart all around us, we have a God to lead us to a resolve. Why we are headed to Death Row is of little consequence. If we had no God we would all be there. And then what would we do? Be thankful, bless God, and pray daily. God will lead you away from Death Row, just ask Him!

In this story, Charlie and Bruce now have the options to turn their world upside down, come close to God, and minister to their new friends. While there is always the possibility of 'The End', thank God there is a better possibility called 'The Beginning'.

# THE END

# OR

# THE BEGINNING!

The end

or

the beginning!